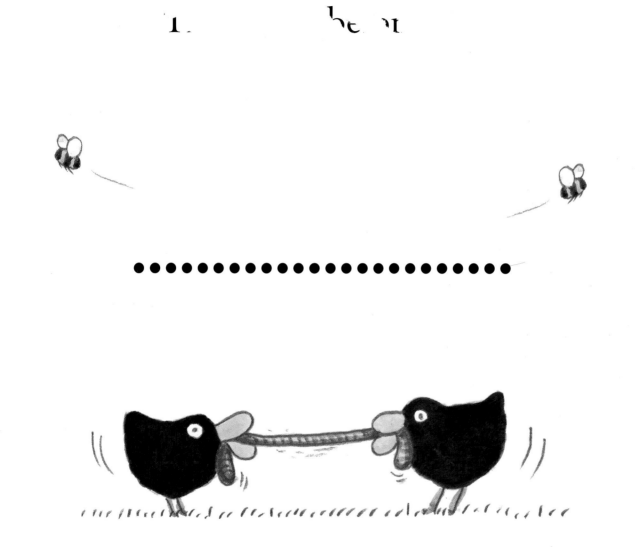

# For Zeki

Dorling **DK** Kindersley

LONDON, NEW YORK, SYDNEY, DELHI, PARIS,
MUNICH and JOHANNESBURG

First published in Great Britain in 2000
by Dorling Kindersley Limited,
9 Henrietta Street, London WC2E 8PS

2 4 6 8 10 9 7 5 3 1

Text and illustrations copyright © 2000 Siobhan Dodds
The author's and illustrator's moral rights have been asserted.

A CIP catalogue record for this book is available from the British Library.
ISBN 0-7513-7268-4
Colour reproduction by Dot Gradations, UK
Printed in China by South China Press

see our complete
catalogue at
**www.dk.com**

# GRUMBLE-RUMBLE!

# Siobhan Dodds

A Dorling Kindersley Book

Little Roo didn't want her breakfast.
She didn't want her kangaflakes, or
her honey on toast.
She wanted to go out to play.

She bounced all around the
garden with her new ball.
Suddenly, she heard a great big
GRUMBLE-RUMBLE!
"A monster!" cried Little Roo, and
bounced off to tell her friend Crocodile.

"There's a monster following me!"
cried Little Roo.
But Crocodile didn't answer.
She was busy eating grapes.

So Little Roo bounced
off to tell Snake.

GRUMBLE-RUMBLE!

"There's a monster following me!"
cried Little Roo.

GRUMBLE-RUMBLE!

But Snake didn't answer.
He was busy munching on an apple.

So Little Roo bounced
off to tell Elephant.

"There's a monster following me!"
cried Little Roo.

But Elephant didn't answer.
He was busy snacking on peanuts.
So Little Roo bounced off
to tell Lion.

GRUMBLE-RUMBLE!

"There's a monster following me!"
cried Little Roo.
But Lion didn't answer.
He was slurping
a milk shake.

GRUMBLE-RUMBLE!

So Little Roo
bounced off to
tell Monkey.

"There's a monster following me!"
cried Little Roo.
But Monkey didn't answer.
He was busy chomping on bananas.

GRUMBLE-
RUMBLE!

Just then Little Roo heard the **loudest**, most **enormous**, GRUMBLE-RUMBLE!

She was so frightened she bounced off home as fast as she could.

"Mummy! Mummy! There's a horrible monster following me!" cried Little Roo. And sure enough there was the **loudest** GRUMBLE-RUMBLE! ever.

"That's not a horrible monster!" laughed Mummy Roo.

"That's your hungry tummy!
Would you like your kangaflakes now?"

"Yes please!" said Little Roo.

And she ate them ALL up!

# Other Toddler Books to collect: